D0789681

Coming Clean

Coming Clean

Kevin Elyot

faber and faber
LONDON·BOSTON

First published in 1984
by Faber and Faber Limited
3 Queen Square London WC1N 3AU
Filmset by Wilmaset Birkenhead Merseyside
Printed in Great Britain by
Whitstable Litho Ltd., Whitstable, Kent
All rights reserved

All professional and amateur rights in this play are strictly
reserved and applications for permission to perform it must be
made in advance to Margaret Ramsay Ltd, 14a Goodwins
Court, London WC2N 4LL.

British Library Cataloguing in Publication Data

Elyot, Kevin
Coming clean.
I. Title
822'.914   PR6055.L/
ISBN 0–571–13228–6

Library of Congress Data has been applied for.

Dedicated to Jack Babuscio

Characters

TONY	About 33
WILLIAM	About 36. From Bradford
GREG	About 38. From New York
ROBERT	About 25
JÜRGEN	About 38. From Hamburg

Setting

The living-room of a first-floor flat in Kentish Town. The essentials are as follows: two doors—one leading to the hallway, bedrooms, bathroom, and front door, and one leading to the kitchen; hi-fi equipment and record shelves; a window looking down on to the street; a dining area; a drinks table; a side-table; a sofa and various chairs. The atmosphere is sparse—it has the potential of being tasteful, but lacks the necessary care. It isn't homely, and also not very clean or tidy.

The action takes place from April to October during the present year.

Coming Clean was first produced at the Bush Theatre, London, on 3 November 1982. The cast was as follows:

TONY	Eamon Boland
WILLIAM	C. J. Allen
GREG	Philip Donaghy
ROBERT	Ian McCurrach
JÜRGEN	Clive Mantle

Directed by David Hayman
Designed by Saul Radomsky

The Adagio *of Samuel Barber's String Quartet begins playing. The house lights fade. As the stage lights come up on* TONY *and* WILLIAM, *the music fades.* TONY *is in a dressing-gown, pulling on a pair of socks.* WILLIAM *is rolling a cigarette. On a chair, in a pile, are a pair of jeans and a shirt. A bag of doughnuts stands on the side-table. Late morning.*

TONY: Was it fun?

WILLIAM: No.

TONY: I'm surprised. He looked quite promising.

WILLIAM: I know.

TONY: Big, hairy, brutal, verging on the psychopathic. Just your type.

WILLIAM: That's what I thought. But he wasn't.

TONY: He looked like he ate babies for breakfast.

WILLIAM: He eats rusks for breakfast. Don't let me hold you up.

TONY: I won't.

(*He starts to pull on his jeans under his robe.*)

WILLIAM: The lights in that disco'd put cosmetic surgeons out of business. I thought he was a virile 40, but in fact he's a rather limp 50.

(*He lights the cigarette.*)

And all those monosyllabic grunts he breathed down my ear in the club soon disappeared when we were sat in that taxi. Crystal-clear enunciation—Oxford English, a hundred per cent proof. And he wouldn't shut up. He went on and on about some opera or other. I mean, I'd expected him to talk about lorry-driving, or hod-carrying, or oil rigs. But no—it was all legatos and top Cs! It's not fair, is it? I thought I'd tricked with Steve McQueen, but I ended up with a leather-clad Richard Baker.

TONY: Steve McQueen's dead.

WILLIAM: He'd still have been more fun.

(TONY *goes into the kitchen.*)

11

Honestly, Tony, I reckon some of these guys are
contravening the Trade Descriptions Act.

TONY: (*Off*) What's he do?

WILLIAM: Something in chemicals. He did explain it all to me,
but it went in one ear and out the other. Like the rest of the
rubbish he came out with.

(*He wanders over to the kitchen door to speak to* TONY.)

Mind you, he's obviously well-off. More money than taste.
His flat's horrendous. An emetic combination of Salvador
Dali and the Ideal Home Exhibition. Gallons of dark-blue
paint everywhere, with hundreds of mirrors, and
glass-topped tables, and concealed lighting. He was so
proud of his dimmer-switch. Kept readjusting it to get the
mood just right. I nearly said, the only thing that'd
improve this room'd be a power cut.

(TONY *enters with two mugs of coffee and a jug of milk.*)

TONY: I quite like the idea of dimmer-switches.

(*He puts the coffee and milk on the side-table.*)

WILLIAM: And you couldn't move for all these statuettes of
Michelangelo's *David*. Everywhere you looked. There was
an epidemic of them. And endless plants of every
description leaping out at you from all directions. Like a
Triffid attack. And the bedroom! I tell you, I was
frightened of falling asleep in there in case I woke up
embalmed.

TONY: I knew I shouldn't have gone. I spent a fortune: 90p for a
pint of lager!

WILLIAM: No one was twisting your arm to drink six.

TONY: I felt so uncomfortable. It's such an effort holding your
stomach in for four hours. Black?

WILLIAM: Yes. With a drop of milk.

TONY: It's a beautiful day. You ought to go for a walk. Get some
fresh air.

WILLIAM: My lungs'd collapse from shock.

TONY: God, those windows . . .

(TONY *takes off his dressing-gown and puts on his shirt.*)

WILLIAM: We didn't get to bed till five. He wouldn't stop talking.
And when we did, it was the same old story—he rolled over

12

as soon as we hit the sheets. Talking of which, I think he must have lost the instructions to his Hoovermatic, cos I'm here to tell you, they hadn't seen the inside of it for weeks.

TONY: You fucked him?

WILLIAM: If only to shut him up, but it didn't. He liked talking dirty. Well, that turns me on. Sometimes. But not when he sounds like a Radio Three announcer.

TONY: Did you enjoy it?

WILLIAM: Not at all. It was like slopping around in a bowl of custard. Loose? I expected to find half of London up there. Do you want a jammy doughnut?

TONY: No thank you . . .
(*He checks himself in a mirror.*)

WILLIAM: It's so disillusioning! All these men who give the impression of being such studs, when in fact they're just big nellies who want to get poked. Anyway, I made up for it this morning. I met his lover.

TONY: He has a lover?

WILLIAM: Yes. He'd been out all night, whoring, and he came back while my number was in the shower. So I introduced myself.

TONY: How civilized.

WILLIAM: Yes—I blew him off. Very nice it was too, until we were interrupted. From the state of the sheets, I should have realized—that guy was going to take a quick shower!

TONY: Did he mind?

WILLIAM: He minded. God knows why. They both screw around, but when it's under their noses—well! So fucking hypocritical! I don't know why they put themselves about. They'd obviously be happier living together in a Wendy house, watching the roses grow round the door. So, while they were going at it cat and dog, I thought it prudent to make myself scarce, which I did. And I left without so much as a cup of instant.

TONY: (*Looking at his watch*) Christ, he'll be here in a minute.
(*He starts tidying up: cushions, books, papers, ashtrays.*)

WILLIAM: That's what you're paying him for!

13

TONY: We haven't even met. I've got to make a reasonable impression.

WILLIAM: Cleaning up for a cleaner! It's like wrapping up rubbish before chucking it in the bin.

TONY: He hasn't definitely said yes. I don't want to put him off.

WILLIAM: Well. . . . So what happened to you after I'd gone?

TONY: Nothing.

WILLIAM: I might have guessed. You were on the brink of a sulk when I left.

TONY: Well, it developed into a major depression.

(WILLIAM *attacks a doughnut*.)

WILLIAM: What about the guy in the construction helmet?

TONY: He deigned to look at me once during the whole evening, and his expression made me feel about as attractive as an anthrax spore.

WILLIAM: There were others.

TONY: He was the only one I fancied. Anyway, you know what I'm like. When it comes to the crunch, I get facial paralysis. I can't even smile, let alone speak. I'm not exactly the greatest cruiser in the world.

WILLIAM: Rubbish! I've told you before, all you need is that little glint in your eye and you could get anyone you wanted.

TONY: A little glint!

WILLIAM: Just a hint of a smile around the eyes.

TONY: A hint of a glint.

WILLIAM: That's right.

TONY: Which I don't have.

WILLIAM: Only when you're not concentrating.

TONY: So how do I normally look?

WILLIAM: Fucking miserable.

TONY: Thanks a lot. William, don't you think you ought to use a plate?

WILLIAM: I like men in construction helmets. As long as they don't wear them in bed.

TONY: He did look good, didn't he? So arrogant. God, he could've done anything he liked with me. . . . I wish I could have met him at a dinner party or something. Had a chat, got to know each other a bit. In that situation, I do far

14

more justice to myself, rather than leaning against a
bar, trying to look like Burt Reynolds. Glinting.

WILLIAM: So why do you carry on going?

TONY: Because it's addictive.

WILLIAM: And you enjoy it.

TONY: Well . . . yes. Sometimes. Anyway, I don't go that often.

WILLIAM: You don't need to. I don't think I'd go at all if I had
    Greg to fuck me every night.

TONY: He doesn't fuck me every night. Not after five years.

WILLIAM: He could fuck me every night after ten years.

TONY: You'd soon get itchy feet. One-night stands don't suddenly
    lose their appeal when you fall in love. The prospect of a new
    body's always exciting. Mind you, it is a transitory
    excitement, and it doesn't change my feelings for Greg.

WILLIAM: A transitory excitement. . . . I saw this guy who looked
    so . . . terribly transitory, and he took me back to his place
    and gave me a transitory rogering on the carpet, and after
    we'd spent our lust all over the Axminster, we lay
    transitorily in each other's arms, and he looked into my
    eyes and said, 'How was it?', and I looked back at him,
    somewhat sultrily, and said, 'My God, that was . . .
    transitory!'

TONY: Have you ever considered sending your jaw on holiday?

WILLIAM: Five years! Who'd have thought it? A paragon of
    domestic bliss! A man, a flat, a car, and now—a houseboy!

TONY: He's not a houseboy. He's a cleaner. Actually, he's not
    even a cleaner. He's an actor.

WILLIAM: An actor! No wonder he's a cleaner. I've yet to meet
    an actor who actually acts. And Greg hates actors.

TONY: We're hiring him to clean, not perform. Whether Greg
    likes him or not is irrelevant. As long as he's good at
    cleaning.

WILLIAM: I wonder if he's good at acting.

TONY: Please try not to be too disgusting when he's here. Not
    everyone wants to know about the workings of your insides.
    Or other people's insides, for that matter.
    (*He looks at his watch.*)
    He's late.

(*He lights a cigarette.*)

WILLIAM: So how are you going to celebrate your anniversary?

TONY: What?

WILLIAM: Your anniversary!

TONY: We haven't talked about it.

WILLIAM: You've got to do something.

TONY: What can we do? Greg's such a difficult sod. He hates parties, hates eating out . . .

WILLIAM: Hates paying for it. Tight-fisted bugger.

TONY: We could have dinner here, I suppose. But I'd end up having to do it all, and that's not my idea of a celebration.

WILLIAM: I'll cook for you.

TONY: I wouldn't trust you with boiling the kettle.

(*The doorbell rings.*)

WILLIAM: It's the slave.

TONY: William, please . . .

(TONY *goes into the hall. Sound of front door opening.*)

(*Off*) Hello.

ROBERT: (*Off*) Hello. I'm Robert.

TONY: (*Off*) Tony, Pleased to meet you. Come on in.

(*Enter* ROBERT *and* TONY.)

This is William . . . and William, this is Robert.

(ROBERT *and* WILLIAM *shake hands.*)

WILLIAM: Hello.

ROBERT: Hello.

TONY: William's a neighbour. Well, almost a neighbour. Often pops round. Sort of a . . . permanent fixture, really. Did you find it all right?

ROBERT: Yes. No trouble.

TONY: Would you like some coffee?

ROBERT: Thank you.

TONY: I'll make a pot . . .

WILLIAM: A pot!

TONY: William.

WILLIAM: Yes?

TONY: Would you like some coffee?

WILLIAM: Yes, please.

TONY: I won't be a minute. Do sit down.

(*He goes into the kitchen.*)

WILLIAM: Make yourself at home.

ROBERT: Thank you.

(ROBERT *sits.* WILLIAM *starts a roll-up.*)

WILLIAM: Would you like a roll-up?

ROBERT: No thanks.

WILLIAM: Don't you smoke?

ROBERT: Sometimes. I have the odd Silk Cut, but then only on social occasions.

WILLIAM: Strictly business, is it?

ROBERT: No . . . yes. I suppose it is.

WILLIAM: You don't mind if I do, do you?

ROBERT: No. Not at all.

(*Pause.*)

WILLIAM: I used to smoke Silk Cut. But I found they made me very chesty. I used to wake up with a very tight feeling just here (*pats chest*), and I'd cough and cough, but it wouldn't budge. Nothing'd come up.

ROBERT: Did you smoke a lot?

WILLIAM: About fifty. But then I decided to roll my own, cos I thought it'd make me smoke less.

ROBERT: And did it?

WILLIAM: No. But it's shifted the phlegm. Now when I wake up and have a really good cough, it all comes up. Great gobfuls of the stuff. Much more satisfying than having it sit on your chest all day.

ROBERT: I'm afraid they're too strong for me. Although they do have . . . quite a flavour.

WILLIAM: Yes. (*Beat.*) This stuff's repulsive. Like rimming a camel. Not that I ever have, but I can imagine. I suppose I'm just a glutton for punishment. Do you want a jammy doughnut?

ROBERT: No thank you.

WILLIAM: Well, it's there for the eating. Madam didn't feel like it. She suffers very badly from morning sickness. I wish you would, cos I'll only eat it if you don't.

ROBERT: I'm really not hungry.

WILLIAM: I don't blame you. They're not very nice. I like the

17

sort which are really squidgy, that you bite into and
the jam squirts out all over the place, and drips down your
chin, and gets everywhere. With these, you're lucky if you
find a pinprick in the middle.

(*Enter* TONY. WILLIAM *devours the doughnut.*)

TONY: It won't be long. Are you all right?

ROBERT: Yes, thank you.

TONY: It's quite a mess, as you can see. I'll show you round in a
minute. I'm afraid Greg and I have been pretty slack about
it all. We're both rather . . .

WILLIAM: Filthy.

TONY: We hate cleaning, and any that was done I did. I think
Greg thinks flats clean themselves. And it's all got a bit out
of hand. So . . . I'll just . . .

(*He returns to the kitchen.*)

WILLIAM: Do you like cleaning?

ROBERT: Yes. Yes, I do.

WILLIAM: Mm. (*Beat.*) I don't. I can always find something
better to do.

ROBERT: It's a case of having to. I need the money.

WILLIAM: Are you very domestic?

ROBERT: In other people's houses. I think I'm quite good at it. I
also do the occasional bit of cooking from time to time. All
helps to bring in the cash.

WILLIAM: What else do you do for cash?

(TONY *enters with the coffee.*)

TONY: Here we are . . .

ROBERT: What do you do?

WILLIAM: I'm a proof-reader for Yellow Pages.

TONY: Black?

ROBERT: White, please.

WILLIAM: I wish I could afford a cleaner. One day, I hope to live
in Kentish Town. But for now, the lower reaches of Tufnell
Park will have to suffice. (*To* ROBERT, *about* TONY.) He's
very grand, this one, y'know. He thinks he lives in an After
Eight commercial.

TONY: White?

WILLIAM: Yes, please. Have you met Greg yet? Oh no, of course

18

you wouldn't have. You'll like him . . . Robert. He's very nice, very warm. A most gregarious, outgoing sort of a person. And generous to a fault, isn't he, Tony?

ROBERT: Where's the bathroom?

WILLIAM: You're not sick, are you?

ROBERT: No. I want to pee.

TONY: It's through there. On the right.

ROBERT: Thanks.

(ROBERT *exits into the hall.*)

TONY: William . . .

WILLIAM: I'm off. I've got loads to do. And I want to get some sleep before tonight. I have to look rested and serene if I'm going to score. At the moment I feel like a bucket of horse-shit.

TONY: Cruising again!

WILLIAM: Of course.

TONY: You never stop.

WILLIAM: Well, you know what it's like. Once you've had a taste, you keep wanting more. Like Chinese food. Talking of which, I've thought of a brilliant solution to your anniversary problem. Equity's answer to Mrs Beeton also hires himself out for dinner parties. And I'm sure he's very cheap.

TONY: What makes you so sure you'd be invited anyway?

WILLIAM: To make up the numbers. As ever. The day I'm invited to a dinner party and find an odd number of guests, I'll know I'm loved.

TONY: William, you are loved.

WILLIAM: You sweet thing!

(*They embrace.*)

I'll buy you something really special for your anniversary.

TONY: There's no need. Without you, there wouldn't be one.

WILLIAM: Oh! D'you know, I think I could fall in love with you, if I didn't find you so sexually uninteresting.

TONY: You break my heart.

(*They kiss affectionately. Enter* ROBERT.)

ROBERT: Oh sorry . . .

19

WILLIAM: That's all right. I'm just saying goodbye. Lovely meeting you, Robert. I'm sure we'll meet again.

ROBERT: Yes. Goodbye.

WILLIAM: Tara, Tony. I'll see myself out.

TONY: Bye.

(WILLIAM *exits. Sound of front door opening and then shutting. Pause.*)

So.

ROBERT: So.

(*They smile.*)

TONY: I'll show you round, shall I?

ROBERT: Yes. (*Beat.*) I like your stereo.

TONY: Good, isn't it?

ROBERT: I've always wanted one like this.

TONY: I'll play something, if you like.

(*Beat.*)

ROBERT: Shall we get the business out of the way first?

TONY: OK.

ROBERT: Where's Greg?

TONY: At a conference. For the weekend.

ROBERT: Oh.

(*Beat.*)

TONY: After you.

(ROBERT *notices something behind the sofa. He picks it up. It's Tony's dressing-gown. He offers it to* TONY.)

(*Taking it*) You don't waste any time, do you?

ROBERT: Oh sorry . . .

TONY: No, no. I'm impressed. Shall we. . . ?

ROBERT: Yes.

(ROBERT *goes into the hall, as* TONY *holds the door for him. As* TONY *exits, he throws the dressing-gown across his shoulder.*)

Morning. A vacuum cleaner is heard offstage. GREG *is reading through a manuscript, trying hard to concentrate. Eventually he looks up and sighs with frustration. He sits back. After several seconds, the vacuuming stops. With relief,* GREG *returns to the manuscript. He begins annotating. The vacuum starts up again.* GREG *buries his face in his hands. Then he composes himself, puts his hands over his ears, and attempts to resume his work. The vacuum gets closer. Soon the door opens and* ROBERT *appears, pushing the vacuum cleaner, covering every square inch of carpet with concentrated thoroughness. He doesn't seem to be aware of* GREG. GREG *has sat back from his work and fixes a beady eye on* ROBERT.

GREG: Excuse me.
    (ROBERT *doesn't hear.*)
    Excuse me.
    (ROBERT *looks across, smiles shyly and continues his vacuuming.*)
    Hey!
    (ROBERT *looks across and turns off the cleaner.*)
ROBERT: Sorry?
GREG: Would you mind?
    (ROBERT *looks slightly puzzled.*)
    I am trying to work.
ROBERT: Oh. I'm so sorry. I wasn't thinking.
GREG: Do you have to use that thing?
ROBERT: Oh . . .
GREG: Couldn't you do something else? Elsewhere?
ROBERT: I've only got this room left to do.
GREG: Well, is there anything you could do that doesn't involve noise?
ROBERT: I should think so.
GREG: I don't wanna be difficult, but I'm finding it totally impossible to concentrate.
ROBERT: I'm so sorry.
GREG: There's no need to be sorry. You're doing your job. The

only problem is I'm trying to do my job too.

ROBERT: I could do the dusting.

GREG: Yeah. Do the dusting.

ROBERT: Would that put you off?

GREG: No. That would not put me off. Dusting's fine. (*Beat.*) So long as it's not loud.

(GREG *has returned to his manuscript and* ROBERT *pushes out the vacuum cleaner. He returns with a duster and starts dusting. After a while, he stops, wanting to say something.*)

ROBERT: I'm sorry to bother you again but . . . are you going to be here for the rest of the morning?

GREG: If that's all right with you.

ROBERT: Yes of course, but I was just wondering when I could do the vacuuming.

GREG: Next week.

(GREG *is still working.*)

ROBERT: OK.

(ROBERT *dusts.*)

GREG: I'm sure the carpet will survive.

(*They continue working.* ROBERT *stops and looks across at* GREG. *He's about to speak, then thinks better of it. He continues dusting. He stops again and plucks up the courage.*)

ROBERT: Would you mind if I interrupted again?

GREG: What is it?

ROBERT: Well, I just wanted to say how pleased I am to have met you at last.

GREG: Uh-huh.

ROBERT: Because I've read your book . . . quite a while ago, actually, and I enjoyed it very much.

GREG: Thanks.

ROBERT: It meant a lot to me.

GREG: Yeah?

ROBERT: You see, I come from Shrewsbury.

(GREG *looks blankly.*)

Have you ever been?

GREG: No.

ROBERT: I don't recommend it. It's very dull. I lived there until I was eighteen. And nothing goes on there. Nothing at all.

And I found it very difficult. Being gay. In fact, I
began to think that I was the only gay in the country, let
alone Shrewsbury. But your book made me realize I wasn't.
It gave me a bit of confidence. It really helped.

GREG: Good.

ROBERT: Never looked back since.

(*Pause. He returns to his dusting.*)

GREG: You're an actor.

ROBERT: Yes.

GREG: Ever work?

ROBERT: Oh yes. But it's a bit of a bad time at the moment.

GREG: From what I understand, it always seems to be a bit of a
bad time.

ROBERT: I suppose so.

GREG: Dunno how you do it.

ROBERT: It can be difficult.

GREG: Ever done television?

ROBERT: Oh yes.

GREG: What?

ROBERT: Bits and pieces. Nothing very much.

GREG: You work mainly in theatre?

ROBERT: Well, that's where the opportunities have presented
themselves, so far. Do you go much?

GREG: No. I prefer the movies.

ROBERT: So do I.

GREG: Uh-huh.

(GREG *returns to the manuscript.* ROBERT *dusts. Pause.*)

ROBERT: You're from New York, aren't you?

GREG: Yes.

ROBERT: I've always wanted to go there.

GREG: What's stopping you?

ROBERT: Don't know. Money?

GREG: You should go. It's very exciting. I love it.

(*Beat.*)

ROBERT: Why do you live here then?

GREG: Well, when I'm in London, I sometimes wonder why I
don't live in New York, and when I'm in New York, I
realize why I live in London. (*Beat.*) My work's here. And

23

of course Tony.

ROBERT: Do you go back much?

GREG: Once a year.

ROBERT: Tony's very excited about the autumn.

GREG: Yeah. It'll be his first visit. I'm looking forward to it.

ROBERT: I really must get it together. One day.

(*Beat. He returns to his dusting.*)

GREG: Hey, I tell you what?

ROBERT: What's that?

GREG: Why don't you leave that?

ROBERT: I've hardly started.

GREG: I can't concentrate with you here. I've gotta get this
finished. It's already overdue. (*Beat.*) Leave it till next time,
yeah?

ROBERT: OK.

(GREG *continues working.* ROBERT *goes out and returns, minus the
duster.*)

I'll be going then.

GREG: So long, Richard.

ROBERT: Robert . . . actually.

(GREG *looks up.*)

GREG: Then so long, Robert.

(*Beat.*)

ROBERT: Tony said you'd have my money.

(*Pause.*)

GREG: How much?

ROBERT: Ten pounds.

(*Beat.* GREG *takes out his wallet and hands him ten pounds.*)

Thank you.

(ROBERT *moves to the door.*)

Bye then.

GREG: (*Working*) Goodbye.

(ROBERT *pauses at the door.*)

ROBERT: I'm sorry if I've been a nuisance, but I didn't expect
you to be here. Tony said you usually . . .

(*The phone rings.* GREG *lifts the receiver.*)

GREG: Hello? . . . Hi . . . I dunno . . . about six, I should
think . . . uh-huh . . . so-so. . . .

24

(ROBERT *has gone out.*)
You wanna word with him?
(GREG *looks up.*)
Well, he just . . . hang on . . . (*Shouts*) Robert?
(*Sound of front door shutting.*)
He's gone . . . just now . . . no, I'm not running after
him. . . . Can't it wait? . . . What the hell do you wanna say
to him anyway? . . . I'm sorry . . . look, I really gotta get
on, OK? . . . yeah . . . see you.
(*He replaces the receiver. Beat. He returns to the manuscript. Pause.
He suddenly throws down his pen.*)
Twenty dollars!
(*The* Adagio *of Mozart's Clarinet Concerto starts playing.*)

As the lights come up, the music transfers to the speakers onstage. Evening.
TONY, GREG *and* ROBERT *are sitting round the dinner table. They have eaten the main course. They are drinking wine.* TONY *is smoking. There is an empty, untouched place set for dinner.*

GREG: They're so damned lazy. It's like banging my head against a brick wall. I have to constantly nag to get any work out of them, and when they do get round to handing in an essay, it's like they're doing me a favour, even though it is six months late. And nine times out of ten, the standard is dismal, so I lose my temper, and then they sulk. They're nice enough kids, but I don't understand why most of them are doing the course.

ROBERT: I could never teach.

GREG: I can't tell you how depressing it is standing in front of my classes. They're like the Living Dead, or the Stepford Wives. They just sit there, blankly.

TONY: Maybe you bore the shit out of them.

GREG: I am never boring. I put a lot into it. I just wish they'd give me a little bit back.

ROBERT: It sounds very frustrating.

GREG: I've even resorted to jokes to try and get a reaction, but will they laugh?! Not a glimmer.

TONY: That's because you're not funny.

GREG: Thanks a lot.

ROBERT: What jokes do you tell them?

TONY: He only knows one.

ROBERT: I can never remember them.

TONY: Why don't you tell it, Greg? We could do with a good belly-laugh.

GREG: I'm not telling it now.

TONY: Go on. Robert wants to hear it.

GREG: You won't find it funny.

TONY: I haven't the past fifty times, it's true, but . . .

ROBERT: I haven't heard it.

TONY: We promise we'll laugh, however badly you tell it. Won't we, Robert?

ROBERT: Yes.

TONY: Go on.

(*Beat.*)

GREG: Well, do you know anything about American history?

ROBERT: Bits.

GREG: Like you know the names of the presidents?

ROBERT: Some of them.

GREG: Does Calvin Coolidge mean anything to you?

ROBERT: A little.

GREG: Well, he was president during the twenties. And it's quite interesting that he should have been because the twenties were, culturally speaking, a very exciting, flamboyant decade, and Coolidge was anything but exciting and flamboyant. He kept himself very much to himself. And he was a pretty straight sort of a guy, a traditionalist, and he believed very strongly in the American way of life.

TONY: It's the way you tell 'em!

GREG: If you don't know fuck all about Coolidge, the joke doesn't mean anything!

ROBERT: Please. Carry on.

GREG: Anyway, d'you know who Dorothy Parker was?

TONY: Greg! He's not stupid.

GREG: Listen, one of my students thought she was a tights manufacturer.

TONY: Please tell the joke. The tension's killing me.

GREG: Well, the day Coolidge died, some guy came up to her and said, 'Have you heard the news? Calvin Coolidge has died . . .'

ROBERT: Oh, and she said, 'How can they tell?' (*Beat.*) Is that the one?

TONY: 'Fraid so.

ROBERT: Sorry.

(TONY *goes to the stereo.*)

TONY: Any requests?

ROBERT: Shall I serve the pudding?

TONY: In a minute.

ROBERT: That's dreadful of me.

TONY: Greg. What would you like?

GREG: Whatever.

(TONY *looks through the records.*)

TONY: Well, let me see. There's Telemann, Vivaldi, Handel, Corelli, Bach, Village People. You'd like some Village People, wouldn't you, Greg? You're not going to sulk, are you?

ROBERT: I'm so sorry.

GREG: I'm not sulking.

TONY: Or we could even have some more Mozart.

ROBERT: We could hear the end of that concerto.

TONY: I think we've heard the best of that. I'm a sucker for slow movements.

(*He takes a record out of its sleeve.*)

More Mozart, I'm afraid. But this one's an andante rather than an adagio. I hope you don't find it depressing.

ROBERT: Oh no. I love Mozart.

TONY: (*Putting record on the turntable*) I have to admit, I am indulging myself. I'm suffering from that well-known after-dinner complaint: Melancholia Hirondelle.

(*He places the stylus on the disc: Mozart's Sinfonia Concertante in E flat (K. 364)—Andante.*)

ROBERT: What is this?

TONY: It's here.

(*He hands the sleeve to* ROBERT *and points.*)

That one.

ROBERT: Oh. I haven't heard this before.

TONY: I quite like it. There's a lovely bit that comes up in a minute. A sort of descending . . . tune, that . . . anyway, you'll hear it.

(*He walks behind* GREG *and kisses his head.*)

All right?

GREG: Uh-huh.

(*Beat.*)

TONY: Well, you could have chosen something.

GREG: I'm OK.
   (*Beat.*)
ROBERT: When I was at school, there was this master who . . .
   took me under his wing, you might say. I don't think he
   was gay, but his interest in me was more than academic.
   Anyway, I used to write a lot—poetry and things—and one
   day, I remember, he called me to his room and worked his
   way through a whole load of stuff I'd given him, line by
   line, word by word, until he'd completely eroded my
   confidence. And at the time, I . . . sorry, are you listening
   to the music?
TONY: No. Carry on.
ROBERT: Well . . . at the time, I accepted what he said. I
   believed him. I could see nothing of value in any of it. And
   he said what I should do was forget everything I'd written
   about, and start afresh. Well, the idea was fine, but it's
   easier said than done. And the unfortunate thing was that
   his comments had an effect, in that I haven't written
   anything from that day to this, and I don't think I'll ever
   forgive him for that. And what really makes me resent
   him—which is why I thought of him in the first place—is
   that much later, we were having a chat about music, and I
   said that Mozart was probably the greatest composer who
   had ever lived, and he said I was wrong. He said that the
   greatest composer who had ever lived was Vaughan
   Williams, and Mozart in comparison was merely a brilliant
   technician. This man, who had completely crushed my
   confidence in writing, obviously couldn't tell Stork from
   butter. To dismiss Mozart as a brilliant technician and
   nothing more is a travesty. (*Beat.*) Don't you agree?
TONY: Of course.
ROBERT: I presume you both like Mozart.
TONY: We do. Well, I do.
GREG: So do I.
TONY: You prefer Verdi.
GREG: I like Verdi too. I also like Handel and Vivaldi. And
   Puccini and Bruce Springsteen. But I also like Mozart. I've
   never said I didn't.

TONY: But you don't like him as much as Verdi.

GREG: I don't know why you say that.

TONY: You don't find him as moving.

GREG: He moves me in a different way.

TONY: Greg's an old softy, really. He listens politely to most music, but what actually gets his juices flowing is a big, thumping tear-jerker, with a tune you can whistle to. A snatch of *Traviata* or *Butterfly*, and he's crying like a baby. Isn't that true, Greg?

GREG: No.

TONY: Hard to believe—such a stern exterior.

ROBERT: I've always loved Mozart. Ever since I was twelve.

TONY: Would you regard yourself as having been a precocious child?

ROBERT: No . . .

TONY: When I was twelve, I was into Helen Shapiro.

GREG: When I was twelve, I was having a nervous breakdown.

ROBERT: Really?

TONY: His Catholic upbringing. Wrestling with the concept of limbo, and he cracked up under the strain. Talking of precocious.

GREG: Fucking nuns.

TONY: Poor thing . . .

(*He strokes Greg's head.*)

Sorry, you were saying.

ROBERT: It's not important.

TONY: It is. Go on.

ROBERT: Erm . . .I've forgotten where . . .

TONY: You were saying how you'd always loved Mozart. Since you were twelve.

ROBERT: Oh yes. You see, my piano teacher introduced me to him.

TONY: Good for him.

ROBERT: She was a woman, actually.

TONY: Oh.

ROBERT: I'd asked her who her favourite composer was, and she said it was him. I'd never heard his music, but because I idolized her so much, I gave him a hearing, and liked it.

I'm not saying I completely appreciated it, but I
sensed there was something there, and for quite a few years,
I went round saying how much I loved Mozart, whereas in
fact I suppose I was imitating a love for him. But I knew
that one day I'd really love him. And it was when I was
taken to Covent Garden for the first time, by an aunt, to see
Così fan tutte, that I fell head over heels. It was the moment
of 'Soave sia il vento'. I'd never heard anything so
beautiful.

TONY: Are you sure you weren't precocious?

ROBERT: I don't think so.

TONY: Then maybe your aunt was. Mine used to take me to
Holiday on Ice.

ROBERT: I'll never forget that performance. And in particular,
the moment when that trio started. It was sublime. So
when this master dismissed Mozart as a mere technician, I
was dumbfounded. I find his music deeply moving. Even
sensual. In fact, the most erotic experience I can imagine is
being fucked to him.

(*He sips his wine, wishing he hadn't said that.*)

I'll get the pudding.

(*He goes into the kitchen.*)

TONY: Yes, that'd be lovely.

(*Beat.* TONY *goes to the phone and dials.*)

GREG: What's the point?

TONY: I'll try just once more.

GREG: It's so fucking rude.

TONY: It's not like him.

GREG: I bet he's out cruising.

TONY: He must have forgotten.

GREG: At least he could have phoned.

TONY: If he's forgotten, he wouldn't phone, would he?

(*Holds on, then replaces the receiver.*)

No.

GREG: Great evening.

TONY: Just because he spoilt your joke.

ROBERT: You know what I'm talking about.

TONY: He's a good cook.

GREG: At that price, he should be.

TONY: It's not my fault.

GREG: Of course it's your fault. It was your idea. You asked him.

TONY: He's all right.

GREG: That's not the point. I just don't want him here.

TONY: So if he hadn't done the cooking, who would have?

GREG: Don't be ridiculous.

TONY: I'm not being ridiculous. If Robert hadn't done the cooking, I would have had to, and I didn't want to. Just for one night, I didn't want to. If you weren't so antisocial, we could've gone to a restaurant, or if you weren't so inept, you could have cooked. But you automatically presume that I will.

GREG: I'm too busy.

TONY: You're too busy! I suppose there are no claims on my time. I have nothing to do but house-cleaning and cooking! It's obvious you regard my attempts at writing as no more than a hobby.

GREG: That is not so.

TONY: It is so. You don't take it seriously.

GREG: I'm being practical.

TONY: So am I. The less I have to do around the flat, the more time I can devote to work.

GREG: I don't have an endless supply of money. I have to be careful. Robert is an extravagance.

TONY: He's not.

GREG: Then why don't you pay for him?

TONY: You know why.

GREG: Because you're broke.

TONY: And I'll stay broke if you treat me as a housewife and not give me the support I need.

GREG: I give you plenty!

TONY: I don't mean money.

GREG: And I don't treat you as a housewife.

TONY: Oh, leave it alone! It's boring.

GREG: It's always boring when you know you're wrong!

TONY: And a happy anniversary to you, too!

(*Enter* ROBERT *with four desserts.*)

32

ROBERT: I did four, just in case William turns up.

GREG: He won't.

ROBERT: Well . . .

TONY: Then there'll be more for us! It looks delicious. Doesn't it, Greg?

GREG: Yeah.

TONY: Where did you learn to cook like this?

ROBERT: I didn't learn. I taught myself. I enjoy it. What about you?

TONY: Oh, I'm not very good at it, and I certainly don't enjoy it. But it's a case of having to.

GREG: And what about you, Greg?

TONY: Greg loves cooking, don't you, Greg? Can't keep him out of the kitchen.

ROBERT: Really . . .

GREG: No. He's joking.

ROBERT: Oh.

TONY: I have an irrepressible wit. Forgive me.

(*They eat.*)

This is delicious, Robert. You've done very well.

ROBERT: I'm very grateful. I need every penny I can get.

TONY: It must be very hard being an actor.

ROBERT: It must be very hard being a writer.

TONY: Yes.

ROBERT: How long have you been at it?

TONY: Difficult to be exact. I've always scribbled away, but I plunged myself into it full-time . . . a few years ago.

ROBERT: What did you do before?

TONY: A mind-crushing job in computers. I had to give it up. And I felt I had to put myself to the test as a writer. What's the point of talking about something if you never do it?

ROBERT: I agree. And how's it going?

TONY: OK.

ROBERT: What have you had published so far?

(*Beat.*)

TONY: Oh . . . one or two things. A short story . . .

ROBERT: Really. What was it in?

TONY: Nothing important.

GREG: The *New Review*.

ROBERT: Oh. (*Beat*.) Could I read it?

TONY: If you like. I'll look it out for you sometime.

ROBERT: And what else?

TONY: Why do you want to know?

ROBERT: I'm interested.

TONY: Well, I've written a few articles for a friend who edits this trade magazine . . .

ROBERT: What were they about?

TONY: A variety of things. In the first one I wrote, I took a hard-hitting look at the advances made in the design of typists' chairs, another was an in-depth analysis of the problems of hiring conference rooms, yet another put forward new ideas for things to do at the office party. . . . (*Beat*.) Impressive, isn't it? I hasten to add I wrote them for pocket-money. My real interest is a collection of short stories which I'm trying to finish at the moment.

ROBERT: And what are your chances of getting them published?

TONY: Surprisingly enough, there is a slight chance. (*Beat*.) I know a publisher who's quite interested.

GREG: You can say that again.

TONY: Greg thinks he's more interested in me than my work.

GREG: I know he is.

TONY: He isn't. He actually believes I can write.

GREG: So do I. But it doesn't alter the fact that that guy is a fat, slimy lecher.

TONY: He's not fat.

ROBERT: Do you have an agent?

TONY: What?

ROBERT: An agent.

TONY: No. (*To* GREG) I don't know what you've got against him.

ROBERT: Mine's hopeless.

TONY: Sorry?

ROBERT: He doesn't get me any work. I complained to him the other day that I'd been unemployed for months, and he got quite shirty with me. He told me my availability was my greatest asset. I think I ought to leave him.

TONY: I think you should.

34

(*Beat.*)

ROBERT: So what do you live on?

TONY: Well, I do the occasional bit of temp work . . . and sign on. More wine, Robert?

ROBERT: Gosh, it sounds just like me. You ought to take up cleaning.

(*It dawns on him this might not be his most successful joke.*)

TONY: Wine.

ROBERT: Oh. Yes, thank you.

(TONY *pours, then his own glass. He is about to put down the bottle when he notices* GREG *holding out his glass for a refill. He looks at* GREG, *then pours him a glass.*)

GREG: Thanks.

ROBERT: Cheers!

GREG: Cheers!

TONY: Cheers.

ROBERT: To success . . . and a happy anniversary!

GREG: Yeah . . .

(*They drink.*)

ROBERT: At least with writing, you can do it by yourself. What I mean is you can't act by yourself. You have to wait for someone to employ you. Whereas with writing you can . . . get on with it. Regardless. (*Beat.*) Although it must be difficult.

(*Pause.*)

Do you find it difficult, Greg?

GREG: It depends, It's vital to have a routine.

ROBERT: Five thousand words before breakfast and all that sort of thing.

GREG: Not quite. It's a case of working out a timetable. The days I'm not lecturing at college I devote to writing. It seems to work.

ROBERT: And what about you, Tony? Do you have a similar routine?

TONY: I write when I write.

(*Beat.*)

ROBERT: I envy you. Both. Perhaps I ought to try my hand at it again. (*Beat.*) I read a lot. I've just read *The Woman in White*.

Have you read it?

GREG: Yes.

ROBERT: Marvellous, isn't it?

GREG: I used to think so. But I reread it a few years back, and I didn't like it as much.

ROBERT: Why's that?

GREG: I guess I just changed my mind, that's all. It's happened before. I'd have a first impression of something and go around saying how fantastic it was. But if I went back to it, I'd often find I didn't feel the same. It's important to reassess your opinions. And few people are prepared to. I always suspect those who say, 'I adore so-and-so,' or, 'I loathe what's-'is-name.' The chances are they don't. They just haven't bothered to think about it recently. Like their opinion's locked in a time warp. Intellectual idleness—I guess that's it. It's hard work keeping your mind open.

(*Beat.*)

TONY: (*To* ROBERT) And what other books have you read recently?

GREG: Excuse me.

(*He leaves the room.*)

ROBERT: Is he all right?

TONY: Not as a comedian.

ROBERT: He seems a bit pissed off.

TONY: He's OK.

ROBERT: Would you like coffee?

TONY: I'm fine at the moment. Thanks.

ROBERT: I'd better clear away . . .

TONY: No. Leave it. There's time for that later.

(*Pause.*)

ROBERT: Could I have a cigarette, please?

TONY: Help yourself.

(TONY *offers him a cigarette.* ROBERT *takes one.* TONY *offers him a light.*)

ROBERT: Thank you.

(*Beat.*)

Five years!

TONY: Sorry?

ROBERT: Five years. That's quite an achievement.

TONY: I suppose it is.

ROBERT: Have you lived together all that time?

TONY: Nearly. We moved in together after a month. Well, I suppose I should say, I moved in. It's Greg's flat.

ROBERT: Quick work! Love at first sight!

TONY: For me. It took Greg a bit longer. He doesn't fall in love easily.

(*Pause.*)

ROBERT: Don't you get jealous of each other?

TONY: There's no point.

ROBERT: I would.

TONY: Have you ever had a relationship?

ROBERT: Yes. Once. And the thought of him screwing around would have driven me mad.

TONY: Why did you split up?

ROBERT: He met someone else.

TONY: Oh.

ROBERT: But while we were together, if he'd have felt the need to have other men, I'd have felt such a failure. If I couldn't have satisfied him, then what price our relationship?

TONY: It can be tricky. But infidelity is a fact of life. We both enjoy the occasional one-night stand. We don't do it all the time, and we'd never bring anyone back if the other one was here. Perhaps it's not ideal. But I think it's realistic. I'd much rather have that than be deceitful to one another—pretending we were faithful when we weren't.

ROBERT: I'd find it difficult.

TONY: Well . . . if you believe in someone, then the odd stray fuck shouldn't be a threat. It's just sex. Gratifying the libido. And if that is a threat, then one's belief must be pretty weak to begin with.

ROBERT: I wish I could think like that. I'm too possessive.

TONY: You'd probably cope. Who knows? Each relationship has its own rules. Mind you, I've yet to see one which convinces me that monogamy isn't abnormal.

ROBERT: But it isn't.

37

TONY: Do you know, the only animals that are monogamous are jackals? And they eat each other's vomit. Hardly a good example to model oneself on.

(*Enter* GREG *in a dressing-gown.*)

You all right?

GREG: Yes.

TONY: Good.

ROBERT: I wonder what's happened to William?

TONY: No idea. (*Beat.*) You didn't take to him, did you?

ROBERT: I've only met him once.

GREG: That should be enough.

TONY: He's sweet.

ROBERT: Sweet William!

(*He giggles.* TONY *smiles.* ROBERT *registers* GREG *isn't smiling.*)

TONY: That was a joke, Greg. You see, Robert was using a horticultural analogy to pun on the names of both the person and the . . .

GREG: Tony, give it a rest.

TONY: Sadly, Americans don't have a sense of humour. They tend to be far too serious about everything. It's all the fault of those fucking Pilgrim Fathers. Dull old cunts . . .

GREG: You know I hate that word.

TONY: No wonder they all mug each other and drop bombs on people.

ROBERT: Shall I make some coffee?

GREG: Not for me.

TONY: I'd love some. Thanks.

(*As* ROBERT *rises, the doorbell rings. Freeze. Then* TONY *gets up,* ROBERT *picks up a few dishes, and exits into the kitchen.*)

Better late than never, I suppose.

(*He exits into the hall. Sound of front door opening.*)

(*Off*) William.

WILLIAM: (*Off*) Happy anniversary.

(*Front door closes. Beat. Enter* WILLIAM. *His face is bruised and cut.* TONY *follows.*)

Sorry I'm late. I got held up.

38

TONY: What on earth's happened?

WILLIAM: Nothing. Just a little hitch. I see you started without
   me. I'm only three hours late.

TONY: William.

GREG: Sit down. Like some brandy?

WILLIAM: You think I should on an empty stomach? Oh go on.
   Force me.
   (*He hands a long, oblong package to* TONY.)
   Here's your present. It's basically for Tony, Greg, but I'm
   sure you'll benefit from it in the end. (*To* TONY) It's got a
   battery in it.
   (*He sits.* GREG *gives him a glass of brandy.*)

TONY: William.

WILLIAM: It was only a bit of rough trade.

TONY: Oh Christ.

WILLIAM: He was gorgeous. Absolutely gorgeous.

GREG: Have you phoned the police?

WILLIAM: What's the point?

TONY: Your face . . . I'll take you to the hospital.

WILLIAM: I don't need to.

TONY: Why didn't you phone?

WILLIAM: It's tricky in a pair of handcuffs. He wouldn't even let
   me answer the phone. That was the worst thing—I can't
   bear not knowing who's ringing me up.
   (*Enter* ROBERT *with a tray of coffee.*)

ROBERT: Here's the coffee . . . oh . . .

WILLIAM: Hello, Robert. Excuse the face. I slipped with the
   blusher.

ROBERT: Would you like some coffee?

WILLIAM: That'd be nice. Getting their money's worth, are they?

TONY: But why did you bother to come over? We'd have come to
   you.

WILLIAM: I didn't want to miss out on anything. I'd have been
   here a bit earlier, but it took me ages to squeeze out of
   those fucking handcuffs.

GREG: What happened?

WILLIAM: I just popped into the cottage for a tea-time quickie,
   and I couldn't believe my luck when this guy gave me the

39

eye—big, brawny, smothered in leather . . .

TONY: Psychopathic.

WILLIAM: And so we went back to my place. It started out quite
promisingly. He told me to take my clothes off and lie face
down on the bed. Then he put the handcuffs on, and I
resigned myself to a slightly heavier session than I ideally
would have wished for at that time of the day. I was more
in the mood for a light snack than a full meal, if you take
my meaning. But then I began to have my doubts, cos he
didn't do anything. He just stood there. And after a while,
he started muttering under his breath. Saying really nasty
things. And then he started to go through all my
belongings, throwing them all over the place, tearing up
this and that, and he'd go for occasional wanders around
the flat, and then come back in, and threaten me some
more. And I thought, Christ, if it wasn't for you, I could
have my feet up in front of *Coronation Street*.

TONY: But your face . . .

WILLIAM: That was his way of saying goodnight—several belts
across the face. That and smashing my record-player. Oh,
and pissing over the carpet. He stood there waving his cock
around, saying, 'I bet you'd like to suck on this, you filthy
little queer.' Trouble is, I would've.

TONY: For Christ's sake . . .

WILLIAM: He was there for ages. I thought he was going to kill
me. Still, I shouldn't complain. At least he behaved like he
looked.

GREG: I bet he wasn't gay.

WILLIAM: I think you're probably right. Anyway, it's his loss. He
doesn't know what he's . . .

(*Suddenly stops. Beat.*)

TONY: Are you all right?

WILLIAM: (*Very quietly*) I'm sorry.

(*He exits through the hall door.* TONY *follows. Pause.*)

ROBERT: Would you like some coffee?

GREG: No. Thank you.

(*Beat.*)

ROBERT: I suppose . . . I might as well . . .

(He clears more things from the table and goes into the kitchen. GREG *pours himself a brandy. He's undecided whether or not to phone the police.* ROBERT *comes back in, clears more things from the table, and returns to the kitchen. Pause.* TONY *enters.)*

TONY: I think I'll take him to the hospital.

GREG: Yeh. Do you think I should phone the police?

TONY: No. I wouldn't bother. There's not much point now. We'll sort that out tomorrow.

GREG: You want me to come with you?

TONY: No. It's probably better if it's just me.

(Beat.)

So I'd better . . .

GREG: Yeah . . .

(They're looking at each other.)

TONY: *(Quietly)* See you.

GREG: *(Quietly)* Sure.

(TONY exits.)

Night. The room is lit by the street light. GREG *is sitting listening to* 'Soave sia il vento' *from* Così fan tutte *playing quietly on the stereo. He's wearing a dressing-gown. The front door opens quietly. After several seconds,* TONY *walks in.*

TONY: Greg?

GREG: Hi.

TONY: I thought you'd be in bed.

GREG: I couldn't sleep. How's William?

TONY: OK.

GREG: What did the hospital say?

TONY: We didn't stay long enough to find out. There were loads of people in front of us, and William was behaving rather badly . . .

GREG: How do you mean?

TONY: He was trying to chat up one of the orderlies. Are you all right?

GREG: Sure.

    (*Beat.*)

TONY: So I thought I might as well take him home to bed.

GREG: Will he be all right by himself?

TONY: He's out for the count. I gave him hot milk, and Mogadon, and then he asked me to read to him.

GREG: Really?

TONY: Yes. A Barbara Cartland novel. Still, I didn't have to read for very long. The combination of Mogadon and Barbara Cartland is enough to knock anyone out.

GREG: What if he wakes up?

TONY: He won't. And I'll pop round first thing. He's not in that bad a state. Just shaken up. (*Beat.*) Haven't heard this for ages.

GREG: Do you want a drink, or. . . ?

TONY: No, I'm fine.

(*Pause.*)
Actually, I didn't want to stay with William. I wanted to
come back here. Spend the night with you.
(GREG *looks at him. He takes his hand.*)
Did Robert get off OK?

GREG: Yeah.

TONY: Did you give him his cab fare?

GREG: Sure.

TONY: I bet he had to remind you.

GREG: He didn't give me a chance to forget.

    (TONY *goes over to the stereo.*)
Next year, just the two of us. OK?

TONY: OK.

GREG: Even if it means a take-away.

    (TONY *puts the record back in the sleeve.*)

TONY: I'm sorry I got ratty at dinner.

GREG: That's OK.

TONY: No it's not. It's ungrateful. I don't mean it. But
sometimes, it's hard to . . .
    (*Beat.*)

GREG: It doesn't matter.

TONY: When Robert asked me about my writing, I felt rather
stupid. I've achieved absolutely nothing.

GREG: You have.

TONY: But it's all so slow. I see you churning out one thing after
another, while I just sit around . . .

GREG: There's no comparison. I'm doing something entirely
different from you.

TONY: And some days, I feel I have nothing to say, nothing
worth writing . . .

GREG: So do I. It's hard work.

TONY: Yes, I know.
    (*Pause.*)
But it is difficult.

GREG: It's late, baby. Why don't we go to bed?

TONY: In a minute.
    (*He goes to the sofa and settles between Greg's legs.*)
Happy anniversary.

GREG: That was yesterday.

(*Pause.*)

TONY: When you arrived at that party, I thought to myself, 'I am going to get that man, if it's the last thing I do.' And I dragged you out into the garden, away from everyone, and sweated blood trying to think of things to talk about. But you didn't give an inch. You're such a difficult bastard.

GREG: God, that party.

TONY: It was pretty awful, wasn't it? I didn't want to go, but William insisted. And I'm glad he did, cos otherwise . . .

(*Beat.* GREG *strokes Tony's hair.*)

GREG: I thought you dragged me into the kitchen.

TONY: Then suddenly, I noticed a little gleam in your eye, and you smiled, and brushed my hand. And I knew it wasn't accidental. And it was at that moment that I thought: 'I've got him!' It was a pity the sex was so disastrous.

GREG: You behaved like a virgin.

TONY: I was tense! And if you remember, you threw up in the bathroom.

GREG: At least it wasn't in the bedroom.

TONY: I might not be able to turn men's heads, but I can certainly turn their stomachs.

GREG: I'd drunk too much.

TONY: Oh, I wish we were going away sooner.

GREG: It's not that long.

TONY: Five months . . .

GREG: Four.

TONY: Well . . . I wish we were going tomorrow. You've got to take me everywhere. I want to go to the Empire State Building . . .

GREG: Maybe.

TONY: And the Statue of Liberty . . .

GREG: Well . . .

TONY: We've got to!

GREG: I've already decided the places we're going to go.

TONY: Where?

GREG: Lots of places! I wanna show you where I lived as a kid . . . there's a little place nearby called Carl Schurz Park, looking out over the East River . . . I spent a lot of time there . . . go to Central Park and take you out on Rowboat Lake . . . Bethesda Fountain on a Sunday. I'll take you to the promenade on Brooklyn Heights, in the middle of the night, and look out over Manhattan . . .

TONY: Is that where Woody Allen and Diane Keaton sat when they. . . ?

GREG: No. And I'll take you to the Village . . . Christopher Street. We gotta go there. And . . . oh, I'll take you places. I'll show you New York. Screw the Statue of Liberty!
(*Pause.*)

TONY: Greg.

GREG: Yeah?

TONY: You must fuck me tonight. We must have an Anniversary Fuck. And you absolutely mustn't take 'no' for an answer.
(*Beat.* GREG *leans down to him,* TONY *moves up to him, and they kiss.*)

GREG: It's very late. And I'm very tired.
(*They kiss again, then* TONY *nestles into his lap. Pause.*)

TONY: If you want to get rid of Robert, I'll understand. Honestly. I won't mind.

GREG: We'll talk about it some other time.
(*He strokes Tony's hair.* TONY *turns into Greg's lap. He opens his robe slightly and begins to blow him off.* GREG *leaves his hand resting on Tony's head and his eyes close. He moans quietly. Suddenly,* TONY *stops. They are both completely still. Then* TONY *raises his head and gently slides round into his previous position between Greg's legs.*)

TONY: Maybe you're right. It is a bit late.

Afternoon. TONY *is sitting at the table, surrounded by pieces of paper and notebooks. He is sharpening pencils.* WILLIAM *is sitting on the sofa, eating a huge cream cake. They both have mugs of tea.*

TONY: It was a miserable evening.

WILLIAM: I thought you were enjoying yourself.

TONY: How would you know? You deserted me as soon as we arrived.

WILLIAM: I wanted to get straight down to business.

TONY: I'm giving up discos. I don't see the point any more. Everyone standing around, trying to look cool and disinterested. End up looking lobotomized.

WILLIAM: The cabaret was fun.

TONY: The cabaret was disgusting. Unamusing, unentertaining, mindless, sexist crap. Repressive drivel!

WILLIAM: You go to discos to be political?! No wonder you have such a good time!

TONY: Simply because I'm surrounded by attractive men, deafened by loud music, blinded by the strobe . . . just because they offer the possibility of a fuck doesn't exempt them from criticism. Not in my book, anyway.

WILLIAM: Have an éclair. Calm yourself down.

TONY: I'm not hungry.

WILLIAM: Well, if I had to choose between political principles and discos, it'd be discos every time.

TONY: That's because you haven't got any political principles.

WILLIAM: I have. I've always been vaguely left-wing. Ever since I had a crush on Tariq Ali. But I can't bring myself to join any party. I've looked through hundreds of manifestos . . .

TONY: Hundreds!

WILLIAM: I have! And if gays are mentioned at all, it's usually ninety-seventh down on the list of priorities. I reckon

46

there's as much homophobia among Socialists as
anyone, made worse by the fact that they won't admit to it.
I prefer downright hostility to hypocrisy. I mean, if I lived
in Teheran, as opposed to Tufnell Park, there'd be no
mistaking what people thought of me. If you're buried up
to your neck in the ground, having boulders hurled at your
head, at least you know where you stand. By the way, who
was that little guy you were talking to?

TONY: He wasn't little. He was a dwarf.

WILLIAM: Why didn't you go off with him?

TONY: Because I wouldn't have known what to do with
him—whether to fuck him, or sit him on the pillow next to
my Teddy Bear.

WILLIAM: Tony! If I didn't know you better, I'd say you were
becoming bitter and twisted.

TONY: I'm fed up.

WILLIAM: Why?

TONY: I don't know.

WILLIAM: Is it your writing?

TONY: Well, that's always a problem. Mind you, I've just
finished a story.

WILLIAM: Have you?

TONY: Yes. This morning.

WILLIAM: I want to read it.

TONY: You can't.

WILLIAM: Why not?

TONY: Not until Greg's read it, anyway.

WILLIAM: What do you want to give it to him for? He'll only tear
it to pieces.

TONY: But that's what I need. Greg knows what he's talking about.

WILLIAM: You have to say that.

TONY: I don't.

WILLIAM: And it's right that you should. It's very loyal. Wrong,
but loyal. Are you missing him?

TONY: He only went yesterday! And he's coming back tonight.

WILLIAM: I reckon what you need is a good fucking.

TONY: I had a 'good fucking' two nights ago.

WILLIAM: Well then, you've got no reason to be fed up.

47

(*Beat.*)

TONY: Actually, it wasn't so good.

WILLIAM: How do you mean?

TONY: I had to ask him to stop.

WILLIAM: I bet Greg wasn't too happy about that.

TONY: He's used to it.

WILLIAM: I've told you before, if you don't give your man your cherry . . .

TONY: It's easy for you. You've got a cast-iron arsehole. Mine's very sensitive.

WILLIAM: Temperamental, more like. It's all in the mind. You can take it if you really want it.

TONY: I know I can. But that doesn't always help. He can use a ton of grease, and it's agony. And other times, with only a dab of spit, I've opened up a mile and felt ecstatic. Stupid, isn't it? Still, he's always been very patient with me.

WILLIAM: Then what are you worried about?

TONY: Because I feel inadequate. As if I'm failing him. I suppose I'm terrified of losing him.

WILLIAM: Losing him? Do you think Greg's likely to leave you because occasionally your arsehole's a bit tight? After five years? I've never heard such rubbish!

TONY: I can't help how I feel.

WILLIAM: Well, if you're so worried, why not do something about it? Practise on the vibrator I bought you.

TONY: I do, sometimes. I used it last night, actually. But I got a complaint from the woman downstairs.

WILLIAM: Why?

TONY: Well, I put it on the floor, impaled myself on it, switched it on, and the next thing I knew, she was hammering on the front door, and said would I please be more considerate and not use the Hoover at such a late hour.

WILLIAM: You need a silencer.

TONY: Anyway, I don't like vibrators very much. I'm very grateful; don't think I'm not. But . . . well, you can't talk to them. They don't whisper sweet nothings into your ear. And you certainly can't suck them.

WILLIAM: You should broaden your horizons.

48

TONY: I suppose I just don't get turned on by throbbing plastic.

WILLIAM: You're too romantic. That's your trouble.

TONY: I am. You're right.

(*Pause.*)

WILLIAM: Have you heard from Robert?

TONY: Not a word. He's too busy being successful.

WILLIAM: When's his series come out?

TONY: Oh, not for ages. He won't have finished filming it yet. Lucky sod.

WILLIAM: Well, it solved the problem for you. You didn't have to go through the messy business of sacking him.

TONY: True. But the flat's not getting any cleaner.

WILLIAM: I've noticed. Still, what's it matter, if it's stopped Greg moaning on about the extravagance. (*Beat.*) You know, dirt's never bothered me. I'd be happy living in a pigsty, if I was sharing my slops with someone I loved. Good orgasms are much more important than clean surfaces, don't you think?

TONY: Maybe.

WILLIAM: I thought it was unnecessary hiring Robert in the first place. I've always suspected couples who live in spotless flats. It's like they're compensating for something—all bra, and no tits. But you walk in here and you think . . .

TONY: All tits, and no bra.

WILLIAM: Yes. You know there are more important things going on than squirting Pledge all over the place, or wiping down the rubber plant. You love each other. That's what's important. Not how versatile you are with a duster. And I tell you, so many people envy you.

TONY: What on earth for?

WILLIAM: Cos you've got it sussed. You're both happily married, you both fuck around, and it doesn't bother you. How many people do you know who cope with that?

TONY: Quite a few, I should think.

WILLIAM: Sometimes I wish I was in your position. Don't get me wrong—I'm quite happy. But there are times when I'd like a bit more. A chance to get to know someone in a relationship. Stability, I suppose.

TONY: Why presume a relationship provides that?

WILLIAM: And occasionally—not often—but occasionally, a one-night stand can be a real downer, when you suddenly catch a glimpse of what that person's really like. I wonder what impression I give? (*Beat.*) Still, most times it's fun.

TONY: You make us sound like an ideal couple. We're not too ideal at the moment.

WILLIAM: How do you mean?

TONY: Well . . . we're not getting on too brilliantly. Greg's a bit cool with me. And we're not making love as often as we used to. Actually, I'm a bit worried.

WILLIAM: If you've been together for five years, you can't expect every day to be magic, can you? You go through phases. You have to have your ups and downs. Changes, even.

TONY: I suppose so.

WILLIAM: You're probably over-reacting. As usual. Always worrying over nothing, you daft sod!

TONY: Maybe. I'm just down at the moment—you know what I'm like. As you say, it's probably just a phase.

WILLIAM: Why don't you plan a wonderful weekend together? Eat yourselves stupid, get pissed, and fuck twice an hour.

TONY: Unfortunately, I can't. I've got to go away this weekend. To a family christening. Actually, I think that's what's depressing me. I loathe family occasions.

WILLIAM: Then what about tonight? Make it really special. Cook him his favourite meal, put candles on the table, have a really romantic evening. Tell you what, I'll help you shop—I love spending other people's money. When's he due back?

TONY: About eight.

WILLIAM: Well, when he walks in, have that piece of music playing—you know, the dreary piece, the one that you both call 'our tune' . . . the Barbirolli . . .

TONY: Barber.

WILLIAM: That's right. Have that playing and drape yourself across the sofa in a jockstrap. Get it just right for when he arrives. Oh, I can see it now! It'll do you the world of good. And by tomorrow morning, you won't know what you've been worrying about! I reckon I've got more faith in you both than you have.

50

*Evening. Light from the street and through the hall door, slightly ajar.
The* Adagio *from Barber's String Quartet is playing on the stereo.
Occasional distant moans from the bedroom. The phone rings.*

GREG: (*Off*) Shit.

    (*Movements off. A door opening.*)

    (*Off*) OK, OK . . .

    (*Enter* GREG, *awkwardly pulling on a dressing-gown. He switches
on a lamp. As he's about to lift the receiver, the phone stops
ringing.*)

    Great! Jesus . . . if you're gonna interrupt a fuck, at least
have the courtesy to wait. Who the hell hangs on for eight
rings?!

    (*He goes into the kitchen, talking the while.*)

    I always let it ring at least ten times. At LEAST ten times!
Jesus . . . you have to allow for people who don't have
extensions, for Chrissake. You have to allow for people
screwing, or taking a crap. You can't expect everyone to be
sitting on top of the goddamn phone.

    (*By now, he's back in the room at the drinks table, with two glasses
with ice in them.*)

    You wanna drink?

    (*No reply. Raising voice*) I said, d'you wanna drink?

    (*Enter* ROBERT, *naked.*)

    Oh, you're here . . . I'm fixing a drink. D'you want one?

ROBERT: Yes.

    (*He sits on the sofa.*)

    Thank you. Who was it?

GREG: Didn't hang on long enough for me to find out. How
many times do you let a phone ring before hanging up?

ROBERT: Oh . . .

GREG: You gotta let it ring at least ten times. At least! That's
only reasonable.

51

(*Hands him drink.*)

Baby, you'll catch your death of cold.

ROBERT: Turn the heating on, then.

GREG: It's not cold enough yet. November, I'll turn it on.

ROBERT: Then I'll catch my death of cold.

GREG: Then wear a robe! It's cheaper.

ROBERT: Haven't got one.

(GREG *sighs with impatience and exits through the hall door.*
ROBERT *walks to the window. He stands to the side, looking
down into the street, sipping his drink. Enter* GREG
carrying a dressing-gown. He notices ROBERT *at the
window.*)

GREG: You ever thought that might be a little indiscreet. . . ?
(*He walks up behind* ROBERT *and wraps the robe around his
shoulders. Then he puts his arms around him.* ROBERT *rests his head
back against Greg's face.*)

ROBERT: I'm sure this smells of me by now.

GREG: He doesn't notice. He wears too much scent.
(*Beat.*)

ROBERT: Our first weekend together.

GREG: Uh-huh.

ROBERT: I've always hated Sunday nights. I think it's a
hangover from schooldays. The prospect of Monday
morning. Back to reality. My father always woke me up at
seven-fifteen, with a cup of tea. I hated it. It was very sweet
of him, but I hated it.

GREG: Would you mind if I turned this off? It's like a fucking
funeral.
(GREG *takes the stylus off the record.*)

ROBERT: I can't bear the thought of tomorrow morning.

GREG: It's still only eight o'clock.

ROBERT: When's he due back?

GREG: Not until lunchtime.

ROBERT: So I leave . . .

GREG: Ten o'clock.

ROBERT: Ten o'clock. That leaves us fourteen hours. Well, I'm
not working tomorrow, so I don't need much sleep. In fact, I
don't need any. So assuming we make it twice an hour, you

52

can fuck me twenty-eight times between now and then.

GREG: I *am* working tomorrow, and I *do* need sleep.

(*They kiss.*)

But not that much.

ROBERT: This is such a treat. Makes a change from snogging in the lavatory of the British Museum, or screwing round at my place at nine-thirty in the morning, or having a quick one here while Tony's in Tesco's.

GREG: Are you complaining?

ROBERT: No. Well, a bit. It is difficult, at times. (*Beat.*) I was defending you the other day.

GREG: Oh?

ROBERT: I was having lunch with this actor, who plays the lead in the thing I'm doing. He's very nice. We get on well. Quite attractive, actually. Unfortunately, he's irredeemably straight. Anyway, he was asking me about myself, and said, did I have anybody, and I said, yes. And he asked if I lived with this person, and I said, no, and he wanted to know why not. So I told him that my lover lived with somebody else, and didn't want to leave him. And he said, but if he loves you, why does he still live with this other person? And I said, because he loves him as well. And he said, but you can't love two people, and I said it would appear that you could. He was quite put out by this. He reckoned that I was getting a raw deal, and that this lover of mine was obviously a two-timing, greedy bastard. (*Pause.*) That's when I attempted to put up a defence on your behalf, but I wasn't very convincing. It's very difficult explaining about us. You invariably come out of it looking like a shit, and I come out of it dripping behind the ears.

GREG: Is this actor guy married?

ROBERT: Oh yes. Of course, the irony is that he hasn't left a vagina intact within a four-mile radius of the studios. The odd deceitful fuck's all right, but falling in love—that's really bad.

GREG: Did it bother you—what he said?

ROBERT: Only to the extent that I don't like to hear you being slagged off. I'll keep my mouth shut from now on. People

don't understand. Why should they? Only those
involved know what's really going on.

GREG: I am a shit.

(*Beat. He smiles. Then* ROBERT *smiles.*)

But I'm not a liar. I love you, Robert. I wish I could
make it easier. But I don't know how.

(*Pause.*)

ROBERT: From the very first moment I saw you, I wanted you.
But I didn't think I had a hope in hell of getting you.
Now I have, I'm prepared to put up with anything to
keep you.

(*Pause.*)

GREG: What say you take off that robe?

(*Pause.*)

ROBERT: What say I do?

(*Beat.*)

GREG: Get one of those cushions—put it on the floor.

(*Beat.*)

Kneel down. Then lie down over it. With your ass in the
air. Slowly. And see what I won't do to you.

(*Beat.* ROBERT *sips his drink. Then he kneels on the floor,
positions a cushion, lets his robe slip to the floor, and slowly
lowers himself over the cushion.* GREG *looks at him. Then
he kneels over* ROBERT *and kisses his back and buttocks. He
buries his face in the side of his back and growls.* ROBERT
giggles.)

ROBERT: So—what won't you do to me?

(*Sound of front door opening.* GREG *and* ROBERT *freeze. Front
door shuts.* GREG *and* ROBERT *leap to their feet and awkwardly
attempt to get Robert's dressing-gown back on.* GREG *goes towards
the door, but turns in his tracks as it opens and* TONY *enters. He
turns on the lights. He is carrying an overnight bag and a carrier
bag. He stops as he notices* ROBERT, *who's holding the robe around
him, untied. A moment of stillness.*)

TONY: Hello, Robert.

(*Beat.*)

ROBERT: (*Just audible*) Hello, Tony.

(*Pause.*)

54

TONY: How's the series going?

ROBERT: Oh, it's . . . (*Tailing off.*)

(*Beat.*)

TONY: Look, I tell you what . . . I'll go and . . .

(*He turns towards the door, stops, turns back and looks at* ROBERT. *Beat.*)

. . . suits you better than it does me.

(*He walks out.*)

ROBERT: My clothes are in the bedroom.

GREG: I'll go fetch them.

(*He exits.* ROBERT *picks up the cushion and puts it back on the sofa. He's not sure what to do. He drains the remains of his drink. Enter* GREG *with Robert's clothes and bag.* ROBERT *hurriedly starts dressing.*)

ROBERT: There's all my stuff in the bathroom. Would you . . . er . . .

GREG: Yeh.

(GREG *exits.* ROBERT *continues dressing.* GREG *returns with a toilet bag. He puts it in Robert's bag.*)

Was there anything else?

ROBERT: I don't think so. No.

(*He finishes dressing. He puts his bag over his shoulder.*)

Will you phone me?

GREG: Yeah.

ROBERT: Tomorrow morning?

GREG: Sure.

(ROBERT *goes towards the door.* GREG *stays where he is.* ROBERT *stops before exiting. He goes back to* GREG, *quickly kisses him on the cheek, and walks out. Pause.* GREG *goes to the drinks and pours out two. Enter* TONY *with the carrier bag.*)

I've fixed you a drink.

TONY: Thank you.

(*He puts the carrier bag on the table and starts unpacking.* GREG *takes the drink to him.*)

GREG: More booty, huh?

TONY: It's getting embarrassing. I keep telling her not to, but she insists. I reckon she'll still be giving me food parcels when I'm 65.

GREG: She's very generous.

TONY: Yes.

(*He looks into an aluminium packet.*)

Look at this . . . a joint of beef. She can't afford it.

(GREG *idly inspects a jar which* TONY *has unpacked.*)

That's from Aunty Ruth. Gooseberry jam. She grows them on her allotment.

(*He takes a few things into the kitchen.*)

GREG: Bad weekend, huh?

TONY: (*Off*) Pretty bad.

(*He comes back in.*)

Actually, it was the worst ever. I've had an awful time. I couldn't face the thought of staying another night, so I made up a rather weak excuse . . .

(*He lights a cigarette and sips his drink.*)

GREG: How was the christening?

TONY: It was . . . OK. I imagine. I've never been to a Catholic one before, so I've nothing to compare it with. All my relatives looked pretty glum, and the other lot—the Catholics—looked pretty smug. And I guess I looked fairly indifferent.

(*He starts taking out more things from the bag.*)

GREG: Is your mother all right?

TONY: She's fine. Thank you. Sends her love.

GREG: That's nice.

TONY: (*Holding up a packet of biscuits*) Chocolate chip cookies. She knows you like them.

GREG: Tony, I'm terribly sorry. I wouldn't have wished this on you for the world.

TONY: The fucking baby wouldn't stop crying. Ugly little tyke. Mind you, I pity him. Having those two as parents. Chances are, he'll end up taking after them, or looking like them . . . or both, God forbid. If I'd have been him, I'd have dive-bombed straight into the font and had done with it. Did you have a good weekend?

GREG: Please . . .

TONY: Try as I might, I can't like any of them. And yet there's a bit of me that envies them. Funny, isn't it?

(*He takes out a cake tin—the final item.*)

Oh—here's the big treat. Again, especially for you.
Chocolate layer cake. 'Greg's Gâteau', as she rather tweely
calls it.

GREG: Thank you.

TONY: I didn't bake it.

(*He takes more things into the kitchen.*)

(*Off*) She's threatening to come up for a weekend. Wants
to see some shows. And she's complaining that you never
go up to see her.

GREG: Let's arrange it . . .

TONY: (*Off*) OK.

(*He re-enters.*)

Well, my weekends are free. How about yours?

GREG: Tony . . .

TONY: What?

(*Beat.*)

GREG: Aren't you going to say anything?

TONY: What would you suggest?

GREG: Well, you can't just ignore it. We've gotta talk about it.

(*Beat.*)

TONY: Do you know, a weekend return is now fourteen pounds,
sixty pence? Unbelievable, isn't it? Fourteen pounds, sixty!
And all for a christening! I think I'll invoice the Pope.
One of the other mob did offer me a lift back—well, as far
as St Albans, but I thought, by the time I've got from
there to . . . Euston. If that's where you go to from St
Albans. Or is it King's Cross? Anyway, I thought by that
time, I might just as well get the Inter-City, especially as
I'd paid the fare, and I didn't really want to have to . . . I
didn't want to have to speak with him all the way. He's
an estate agent. His wife's the shyest person I've ever met.
He speaks for her all the time. She's Cornish. So he says.
Have you always used the flat? Or was it just this
weekend, and the rest of the time you've used his place?
Or do you go somewhere else? (*Pause.*) You do it here,
don't you? In the bedroom, in here . . . everywhere. I've

never noticed any stains. Mind you, he has made a living out of cleaning up. (*Beat.*) So you've obviously planned it very well, cos I've never. . . . Does he watch me leave? Is he hiding somewhere, lurking behind the hedge, and as soon as he sees me turn the corner, he leaps up the stairs, tearing off his jeans for a quickie? Am I right? And all those nights when we haven't made it, was that cos you'd been with him and you'd fucked yourself dry?

GREG: Tony.

TONY: You wanted me to talk—I'm talking. When was the first time? No, don't tell me. The night of our anniversary, wasn't it? Or was it before?

GREG: No. It wasn't before.

TONY: *Così fan tutte.* I thought it rather odd you should be listening to that—you hardly ever play Mozart. Was he right? Is it the most erotic experience you can imagine, fucking to Mozart? Maybe we should try it. A quick blast of *The Magic Flute* and you'd be up me like a rat up a drain. I thought I smelt something on your cock. But I stopped myself saying anything, because I thought well, even if he has, what's it matter? That's the name of the game. He's allowed to. So am I. The occasional bit on the side. All part of the arrangement. But I didn't think that arrangement provided for a . . . four-month affair. It is four months, isn't it? (*Beat.*) Why didn't you tell me?

GREG: How could I tell you?

TONY: You should've told me. It's ridiculous . . .

GREG: Is it? You think I should have told you? 'Hey Tony, I'm screwing Robert, so whadda ya know?' Is that what you wanted? That's what you wanted me to tell you? I think *that*'s ridiculous.

TONY: But the whole point is that we shouldn't have to lie to each other . . .

GREG: The whole point is that we should stick together! And if that means we have to lie to each other, then that's fine by me!

TONY: Don't include me in that. I don't lie to you.

GREG: Oh no, you're so fucking virtuous! So paranoid about the truth. It's not such a big deal.

TONY: You really mean that?

GREG: Yeah.

TONY: Well, I don't believe you. You're kidding yourself. Anything to resist feeling guilty. It is a big deal, and you know it.

GREG: Maybe talking about it's not such a good idea.

TONY: Jesus Christ, it makes me look so stupid! How many people know about this? Does William?

GREG: No. No one.

TONY: Is that the truth?

GREG: Of course.

TONY: Of course! Sorry—I'm just being paranoid.

GREG: Of course it's the truth. No one knows.

TONY: Is he the only affair you've had while we've been together?

GREG: Yes.

TONY: Are you sure?

GREG: For Christ's sake!

TONY: How do I know you're telling the truth? Is he the only affair you've had while we've been together? I want to know.

GREG: I've told you—he's the only one.

TONY: You're sure about that, are you?

GREG: Will you stop this?

TONY: Do you love me?

GREG: What?

TONY: I said, do you love me?

GREG: You're gonna carry on like this all night?

TONY: Answer me.

GREG: Cos if you are, I'm going out.

TONY: I've asked you a question.

GREG: OK, I'm going out.

TONY: (*Barring his way*) Do you love me?

GREG: Get out of my way.

TONY: Do you love me?

GREG: You know I do.

TONY: But really . . . do you love me?

GREG: Yes, I really love you. Now get the fuck out of my way.

TONY: No.

GREG: Tony!

TONY: I want to know if you love me.

GREG: I've told you.

TONY: Do you love him?

GREG: Oh shit . . .

TONY: Do you love him? Tell me.

GREG: Get out of my way, Tony.

TONY: Tell me! Do you love him?

GREG: Move, for fuck's sake!

TONY: Do you?

GREG: Yes.

> (*Beat.*)

Yes, I do.

> (*They are still.*)

TONY: Well, that certainly has the ring of truth.

> (TONY *goes to the sofa and sits.* GREG *stays at the door.* TONY *lights a cigarette. Then he half looks back at* GREG.)

I thought you were going out.

> (GREG *goes to him and puts a hand on his shoulder.* TONY *tenses up.* GREG *takes his hand away.*)

Is he a good fuck? Is he a better fuck than I am? Is that what it is? I bet he is. I bet he's got a really slack arsehole. Hasn't he? I bet he can't get enough of it. Like a cat on heat, waving it around, begging for more. That's it, isn't it?

GREG: No.

TONY: I mean, that's what it basically comes down to, doesn't it?

GREG: It has nothing to do with that.

TONY: And you're prepared to jeopardize our relationship for the gratification of your cock. Because you've found an easier lay than me, you're prepared to ditch us. Who'd have thought that our five years together would eventually stand or fall on the elasticity of my sphincter?

> (*Beat.* GREG *returns to his papers. Pause.*)

60

You can go out if you want to. I won't stop you.

GREG: I don't want to go out.

TONY: You said you did.

GREG: Well, now I don't.

> (*Pause.*)

TONY: I don't feel very well. I feel a bit sick.

GREG: Go to bed, then.

TONY: No. The room'd start spinning. It'd make me throw up. I don't want to spend all night hanging over the lavatory.

> (*Pause.* TONY *looks across at* GREG.)

You're not concentrating on that. You're only pretending to.

> (*Beat.*)

Aren't you?

GREG: I certainly can't concentrate if you carry on talking.

TONY: You wanted me to talk.

GREG: I think it'd be better if we talked tomorrow.

> (*Pause.*)

TONY: Greg?

GREG: What?

> (*Beat.*)

TONY: Are you going to carry on seeing him?

> (*Pause.*)

GREG: Yes.

TONY: I see.

> (*Beat.*)

So that's it then.

GREG: What do you mean?

TONY: I mean, I'm not going to share you with that little jerk. I want you for myself.

GREG: You want me for yourself?

TONY: Yes.

GREG: How can you say that? You've never had me for yourself. And I've never had you for myself. And I don't want that. I don't want that from anyone. We haven't been faithful to each other ever since we met, and we've both accepted that. At least, I have. So why have you suddenly decided you're not in the mood for sharing?

We've shared each other around half the gay scene in London!

TONY: But we haven't fallen in love with half the gay scene in London, have we? They were one-night stands. And that's different from having a four-month affair with a cleaner! You know it is.

GREG: You still think it's just a case of turning a blind eye to one-night stands, don't you? You've never been able to think further than that.

TONY: You seem to have changed the rules somewhere along the line. Since when has it been a case of turning a blind eye to a grubby little liaison . . .

GREG: Changed the rules? What rules? What rules are you talking about? You want rules? You want us to make promises? OK, we'll make promises. So we'll never sleep around again. You'd like that, wouldn't you? You'd like not to be able to go to discos and bars with William, wouldn't you?

TONY: I thought you'd have to bring him up.

GREG: Well, he's not exactly a celibate influence, is he? You think I enjoy the prospect of what you two get up to when I have to go away?

TONY: Brilliant! You're the one who's wrecking our relationship and of course it's William's fault!

GREG: I am not wrecking our relationship! Would you think for one minute! There's always been the possibility that things'd change. And you've never been able to accept that. You've said you can, but you can't. But just because they are changing, it doesn't mean they're coming to an end. We can't chuck the whole thing out!

TONY: I am not prepared to share you with anybody. Take it, or leave it.

GREG: I leave it.

TONY: Fine. That's how much you love me!

GREG: You haven't understood a word I've said.

TONY: I've understood everything.

GREG: You're not even trying.

TONY: You're prepared to give me up, and you're not prepared to give him up. That's all there is to understand! But what you'd really like is for me to say, fine, go ahead, have Robert as well, I don't mind, so that you can have your cake and eat it.

(*He's on his feet, heading for the drinks table.*)

GREG: Oh shit!! You're not making it any easier for me!

TONY: Was that a cry for sympathy? That really is too much to ask! I seem to remember I'm the one who walked into this room not ten minutes ago to be confronted by our ex-skivvy. Why should it be my responsibility to make anything easier? You should be down on your fucking knees, not standing there giving me lectures on how to conduct relationships.

GREG: Tony . . .

TONY: Your teaching credits aren't exactly shit-hot at the moment. Why should I listen to someone who thinks with his cock?

GREG: Tony . . .

TONY: You really are an arrogant bastard! Make it easier for you? Jesus Christ. . . !

(*They embrace, holding each other tightly.*)

The only thing I've ever wanted is to be with you. I could do without anything, as long as I have you. I can't bear the thought of you looking at anyone else, let alone making love to them. Every time I knew you were with a trick, I felt sick. I tried not to think about it, but I couldn't get it out of my mind. That you'd whisper the same things as you whisper to me, moan in the same way when you came, kiss, like you kiss me, after it's all over, and hold him in your arms, and close your eyes. I can't cope with it any more. I'm tired of all the bars and clubs, tired of looking around, of competing, pretending I need other men when all I want is you. Why don't we stop it now? Why don't we start all over again? We don't need anyone else. Sitting here, cuddled up together, making love. That'd be so nice, wouldn't it, Greg? Wouldn't that make you happy? Just the two of us, together? He wasn't even a good cleaner!

63

GREG: (*Still embracing* TONY) You haven't enjoyed me making love to you for the past twelve months . . .

TONY: That's not true . . .

GREG: . . . maybe longer. You used to. It used to be fantastic. But not any more.

TONY: It's just a phase . . .

GREG: Tony . . .

TONY: It is. Relationships go in phases. They have their ups and downs. And we're having a down.

GREG: A pretty long down.

TONY: It'll soon go up again.

(*Beat. They smile.*)

GREG: Tony, it doesn't bother me. But it bothers you. And it shouldn't. It's making you so unhappy. And that touching little domestic scene you describe—I don't want that. I never have. And you know that. I'm not that person. You've got to accept things as they are, not kid yourself they're like they were, or pretend they're what they've never been. I still love you. I still want us to be together. But I'm not suddenly going to ask you to lay out my pipe and slippers. And I doubt that Robert will suddenly disappear into thin air.

TONY: I can but hope.

(GREG *kisses his forehead.*)

It's certainly taught me one thing: from now on, I'll always do my own housework! (*Beat.*) Listen, why don't we have a romantic moment on the sofa? Stuff our faces with chocolate cake, wash it down with a large drink, and listen to our favourite music. (*Beat.*) Yes?

GREG: OK.

TONY: You get the cake. I'll sort it out in here.

(GREG *goes into the kitchen.* TONY *pauses a moment. Then he looks through the records. He can't find what he wants. His search becomes more animated. Then he notices the sleeve he's looking for, lying empty. The record is already on the turntable. As he picks up the sleeve,* GREG *comes in from the kitchen, having suddenly realized something.*)

GREG: Tony . . .

(*He stops as he sees* TONY *with the sleeve.*)

TONY: Obviously, a popular choice.

(*The phone rings.* TONY *leaps to it.*)

If that little bastard dares. . . . (*He lifts the receiver.*) Yes?
(*Beat.*) Oh yes, hello, how are you? . . . no I'm fine,
fine . . . lovely to hear from you . . . you phoned
earlier? . . . ah well, I was out—we were out . . . yes, just
got back in . . . it's going all right—slowly but surely,
yes . . . oh I can't wait . . . yes I know I've left it too long
but . . . it's only a few weeks now . . . I'll see you then . . .
yes . . . yes he is, I'll . . . and to you, yes . . . hang on . . .
(*He holds out the receiver to* GREG. GREG *takes it.*)

GREG: Hello? . . . Mom, hi, how are you? Is anything
wrong? . . . No, everything's fine . . . is Dad OK? . . .
Uh-huh . . .

(TONY *takes the record off the turntable, replaces it in its sleeve,
and puts it back on the shelves as* GREG *continues talking.*)

. . . He won! That must be the first time in his life—how
much? . . . Twenty dollars, huh? Well, it's a start . . . it'll
all go on this call if you're not . . . hi, Dad,
congratulations! . . . yeah, that's great . . . I know she
doesn't approve but . . . you gotta give her some of it . . .
uh-huh . . . well, if it blocks you up, don't eat it, she won't
mind . . . no, no, look this is using up all your money . . .
yeah, we're looking forward to seeing you too . . . Tony's
very excited . . . you're gonna meet us at the airport? . . .
that's great . . . we'll speak before then, OK? . . . love to
Mom . . . and to you . . . yeah, I will . . . bye now.

(*He replaces the receiver. Pause.*)

TONY: I'm going to bed. How about you?

GREG: In a while. (*Beat.*) You want some cake?

TONY: No. I'm not hungry. Thank you.

(GREG *goes to his papers.*)

How long are you going to be?

GREG: Not long.

TONY: See you in a bit, then.

GREG: Yeah.

(TONY *goes to the door.*)

Oh by the way, I read your story.

TONY: You did?

GREG: Yeah.

TONY: I didn't think you'd have had the time.

(*Beat.*)

GREG: It's quite good. (*Pause.*) I think the central character suffers from being too narrowly defined. He needs a certain . . . fleshing out. I didn't quite believe in him as a person. (*Beat.*) I think if you're gonna have a character behave so . . . extremely, you have to have established him sufficiently; you have to . . . deserve, if you like, the taking of that liberty . . . with your material.

(*Pause.*)

You really think I'm like that?

(*Pause.*)

TONY: So you think it's only quite good.

GREG: There are many excellent things in it . . .

TONY: But all these excellent things add up to only quite good.

GREG: Oh shit, Tony, what do you want me to say? It needs more work. You're maybe a little too close to your material. But for Christ's sake, you haven't written that much, so what can you expect? As an early effort, it is quite an achievement.

(*Pause.*)

TONY: Well, thank you for having bothered to read it.

GREG: Oh come on . . .

TONY: No, no, really. I'm . . . quite grateful.

(*Beat.*)

Sorry.

(*Beat.*)

So. I'll get ready then.

(*As he turns to leave, he notices the dressing-gown on the floor. He picks it up.*)

Greg?

GREG: Yeah?

TONY: What you were saying earlier . . . I did understand.

(*Beat.*)

But I really don't think I can . . .

66

(*Beat.*)
GREG: What?
(*Beat.*)
TONY: It doesn't matter.
(*He puts the dressing-gown over his shoulder and walks out, as Voggue's 'Dancin' the night away' starts playing.*)

Voggue fades as the lights come up. Night. The only light spills in from the street through the window. The front door is heard being opened. The sound of people entering and walking along the hall. The door opens. Enter TONY. *He motions in* JÜRGEN, *who is dressed entirely in leather.*

TONY: Kalt.

JÜRGEN: Bitte?

TONY: Ja. Sehr kalt.

JÜRGEN: Ach ja.

TONY: Er . . . möchtest du ein . . . er . . . du möchtest . . . er . . . do you want a drink?

JÜRGEN: Ja.

TONY: Was?

JÜRGEN: Whisky?

TONY: Visky . . . whisky, ja. Yes. Eissen?

JÜRGEN: Eissen?

TONY: Ice . . . brrr.

JÜRGEN: (*Shivers.*) Ja.

TONY: Nein. In the drinken. The whisky.

JÜRGEN: Ach ja. I want . . . straight up. Not on the rocks.

TONY: Ja. Gut.
  (*Starts fixing the drinks.*)
  Du setzest?
  (*He motions to the sofa.*)

JÜRGEN: Bitte?

TONY: Do you . . . er . . . want to setzen?

JÜRGEN: (*Sitting on sofa*) Ich verstehe nicht.

TONY: Bitte?

JÜRGEN: Not understand.

TONY: Oh but you have. You've just done exactly what I wanted you to.

JÜRGEN: Bitte?

68

TONY: Don't worry. Das ist gut.

JÜRGEN: Ja.

TONY: Ja.

(TONY *hands him a drink.*)

JÜRGEN: Zum Wohl!

TONY: Cheers!

(*They drink.*)

Music . . . Musik?

JÜRGEN: Ja.

TONY: What do you like? Was . . . do you like? Disco?

JÜRGEN: Nein, nein. Zuviel Disco . . . quiet . . .

TONY: Quiet. Ja.

JÜRGEN: Und langsam . . . slow.

TONY: Slow. Quiet and slow. I've got loads of that.

(*He chooses a record and puts it on—Schubert's Quintet in C (D. 956:* Adagio.)

Tell you what . . .

(*He produces a small electric fire from a corner and sets it up in front of the sofa.*)

. . . rather than freezing to death . . . the central heating's broken down . . . too fucking mean to have it mended . . . well, that's his problem. . . .

(*He sits next to* JÜRGEN.)

Better? Ja?

JÜRGEN: Ja.

TONY: Gut.

(*Pause.*)

You like this? Musik gut? Ja?

JÜRGEN: Ach ja. Schubert.

TONY: That's right.

JÜRGEN: Sehr schön. Sehr traurig.

TONY: Traurig?

JÜRGEN: (*Trying to explain*) Ach . . .

TONY: Oh, it doesn't matter. I'm sure you're right.

(JÜRGEN *looks across at* TONY. *He chuckles. He slaps Tony's leg affectionately.* TONY *smiles back, although the slap was somewhat harder than he would have liked.* JÜRGEN *drains his glass.*)

69

Another? . . . ein anderer?

JÜRGEN: Ach . . . nein.

(JÜRGEN *puts down his glass and puts his arm along the back of the sofa.* TONY *looks at him.* JÜRGEN *draws* TONY *into him and kisses him. As he does so, he gradually envelops* TONY. *The kiss goes on for a long time. As their lips part,* TONY *is limp with desire.*)

JÜRGEN: Wohnst du hier allein?

TONY: Pardon? Bitte?

JÜRGEN: You . . . live . . . alone?

TONY: No. Well, yes. Sort of.

(JÜRGEN *doesn't understand.*)

I'm alone . . . allein . . . jetzt . . . at the moment . . . my landlord . . . em . . . nicht hier . . . er ist . . . erm . . . on holiday . . . in New York.

JÜRGEN: Ach. New York. Ja. Sehr gut. Grosse Schwänze! Gute Fickerei! Ja.

TONY: Mmm . . .

JÜRGEN: (*Trying to explain*) Big cocks . . . good fucking . . . in New York.

TONY: Yes, I'm sure there is.

JÜRGEN: Ja! Sehr gut! I . . . love . . . New York.

TONY: Anyway, I'm not here for much longer. Ich gehe . . .

JÜRGEN: New York?

TONY: No. Ich gehe . . . from hier . . . next week. Ich . . . move in with . . . a friend . . . mit einem Freunde. Ja! Ich . . . move in with a friend . . . next week. Oh fuck it, it doesn't matter.

JÜRGEN: Ja.

(TONY *kisses him. During the kiss,* JÜRGEN *fondles Tony's crotch and arse. Their lips part.*)

TONY: You, and Schubert—who needs conversation?

JÜRGEN: Bitte?

TONY: You don't understand a word I'm saying, do you?

JÜRGEN: Verstehe nicht.

(*He chuckles and starts kissing Tony's neck. During the following speech, he works thoroughly over Tony's body, and even though* TONY *continues speaking, with hardly any inflection, it obviously turns Tony on a lot.*)

TONY: I could say . . . you're faintly ludicrous . . . you leave
me cold . . . (*Moans with pleasure.*)

JÜRGEN: (*Briefly taking his mouth from Tony's body*) Gut . . . gut . . .

TONY: Ja . . . oh ja . . . if you don't get off me this instant, I am
going to break that glass and rub it into your neck—you
disgust me . . . oh . . .

JÜRGEN: . . . gut . . . gut . . .

TONY: Oh ja . . . mm . . . you think you're so good, don't you . . .
I wonder how many arses you've fucked . . . hundreds . . .
thousands . . . and mine will be one more notch on your
cock . . . if you're lucky . . . oh . . .

JÜRGEN: . . . ja . . .

TONY: Mm . . . I think you once appeared to me . . . during a
wank . . . and very like what I dreamt of . . . when Greg
was making love to me—oh—I could even say I love you.
(*Suddenly* JÜRGEN *lifts his head.*)

JÜRGEN: Was?

TONY: What is it?

JÜRGEN: Du liebst mich? You . . . love . . . me?

TONY: Oh, no! I mean, I like you. But no, I don't love you.

JÜRGEN: Gut! Me . . . no love . . . I don't like.

TONY: No. It is a nuisance, isn't it?

JÜRGEN: I had . . . lover . . . he . . . verheiratet, verheiratet . . .
ach . . . eine Frau . . . woman.

TONY: Went off with a woman?

JÜRGEN: Ja . . .

TONY: How irritating!

JÜRGEN: Und ich . . . ich . . . (*Mimes slashing wrists.*)

TONY: Oh no! It's never worth it. (*Looks for the scars.*) I can't see
any scars . . .

JÜRGEN: Nein. Ich war . . . scare?

TONY: Scared?

JÜRGEN: Ja.

TONY: Frightened. You were too frightened. Thank God for that.
Otherwise I'd have been at a loose end tonight . . .

JÜRGEN: Und . . . now . . . no more love . . . never!

(JÜRGEN *holds Tony's head between his hands and kisses him. He
pulls* TONY *into him. Pause.*)

TONY: You can't say that. I can see why you should but . . . no, you can't say that.

JÜRGEN: 'Ich liebe dich.' Die ganze Zeit, hat er gesagt, 'Ich liebe dich.' Ich liebe dich!

(*He runs his fingers through Tony's hair. Pause.*)

TONY: Ich liebe dich.

(*Pause.*)

JÜRGEN: Schubert hat dieses Stück in seinem letzten Lebensjahr geschrieben, als er nur einunddreissig war. Unglaublich, nicht?

(*Beat.*)

TONY: Now you've completely lost me.

(*Beat.*)

Sorry, I don't know your name.

JÜRGEN: Bitte?

TONY: It's not important.

(*The lights are fading as the music plays on.*)

This is so nice.

JÜRGEN: Gut, ja?

TONY: Oh yes. Sehr, sehr gut.

(*They remain still and close together, in the warm red glow of the electric fire. And, slowly, that fades to black.*)